Brave Lion,
Scared Lion

Brave Lion, Scared Lion

Joan Stimson

Illustrated by
Meg Rutherford

Look out for
Big Panda, Little Panda,
A New Home for Tiger,
and Swim Polar Bear, Swim!
also by Joan Stimson and Meg Rutherford.

Scholastic Children's Books,
Commonwealth House, 1–19 New Oxford Street,
London WC1A 1NU, UK
a division of Scholastic Ltd

London • New York • Toronto • Sydney • Auckland
Mexico City • New Delhi • Hong Kong

First published in the UK by Scholastic Ltd, 1997
This edition published by Little Hippo, an imprint of Scholastic Ltd, 1999

Text copyright © Joan Stimson, 1997
Illustrations copyright © Meg Rutherford, 1997

ISBN 0 590 19900 5
Printed and bound in China

On a far-away plain, near a cool water-hole, lived twin lion cubs. Their names were Jake and Jasper.

As they grew, the brothers would wander to the water-hole and admire their reflections.

"What a brave lion I am!" cried Jake. And he growled and he prowled with pride.

But Jasper kept quiet. Because Jasper was timid and shy. And sometimes he felt scared. He felt scared when Jake chased him up a tree and then he looked down.

He felt scared if Great Uncle Jiggly Jowls bellowed when Jake tweaked his tail.

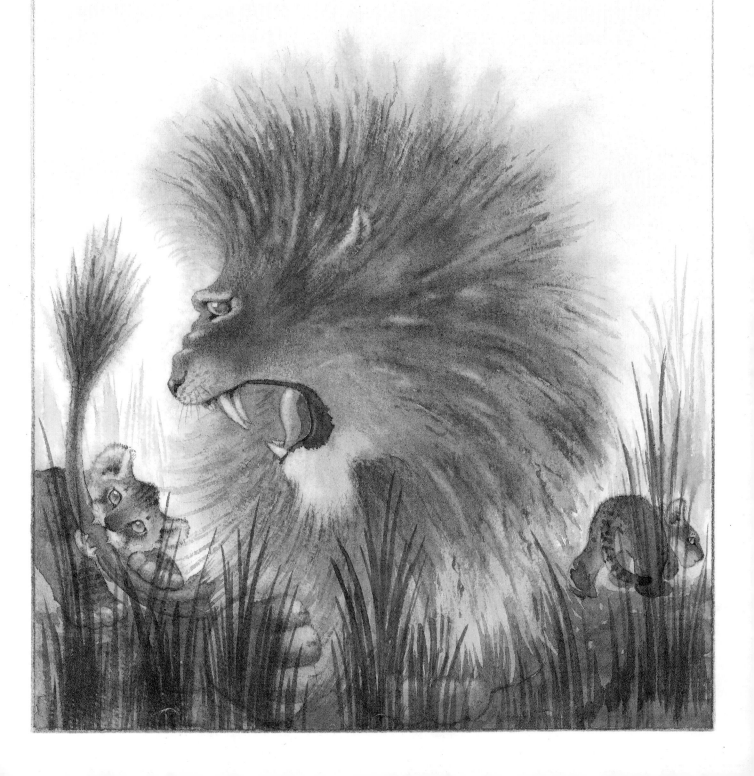

And Jasper *shivered* when Mum took them down to the river. And warned them about crocodiles.

"I wish I could be brave like Jake," sighed Jasper.
But Mum was always ready with the same reply.
"Good heavens! There's more to being brave than
showing off."

Then she would give Jake a playful push.

And lick Jasper gently behind his ears.

One day Jake and Jasper set off for the water-hole. "Don't be long," Mum told them. "And stay well away from the river."

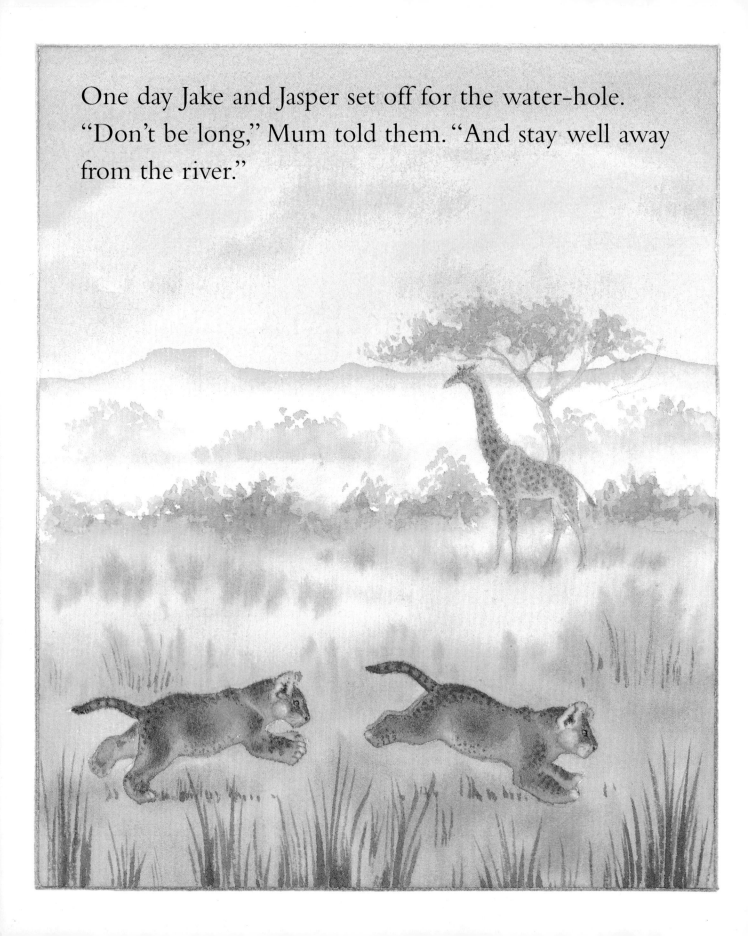

But, when the cubs had drunk and played and admired their reflections, Jake wanted to do something different.

"Come on," he called to Jasper. "I'm going to count the crocodiles."
By the time they reached the river Jasper was worn out and worried.

Jake was disappointed. "There's not a crocodile in sight," he grumbled. So he decided to show off.

"Don't!" pleaded Jasper. "It's dangerous and it's time to go back." But Jake was already dancing from rock to rock and singing. "What a daring lion I am!"

Jake was still enjoying himself when a rock by the far bank shifted and stirred. First a pair of eyes appeared. And then ... a huge mouth.

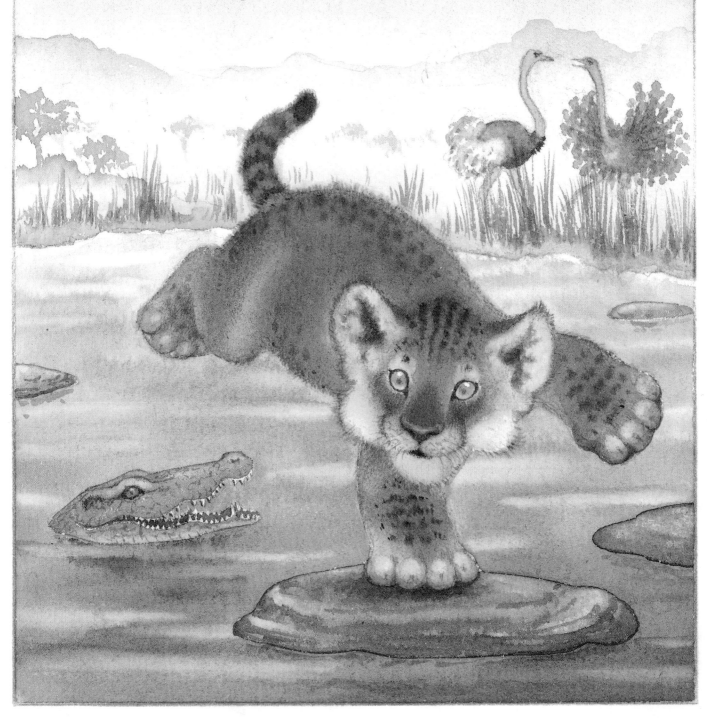

"Watch out," cried Jasper. "It's a crocodile!"
Jake froze in his tracks. He was too terrified to move a paw.

Because suddenly, every rock looked like a crocodile to Jake.

Jasper was terrified too. But he leapt to Jake's side. And tugged at his tail.

The tug brought Jake back to his senses. And with a squeal he hid behind Jasper.

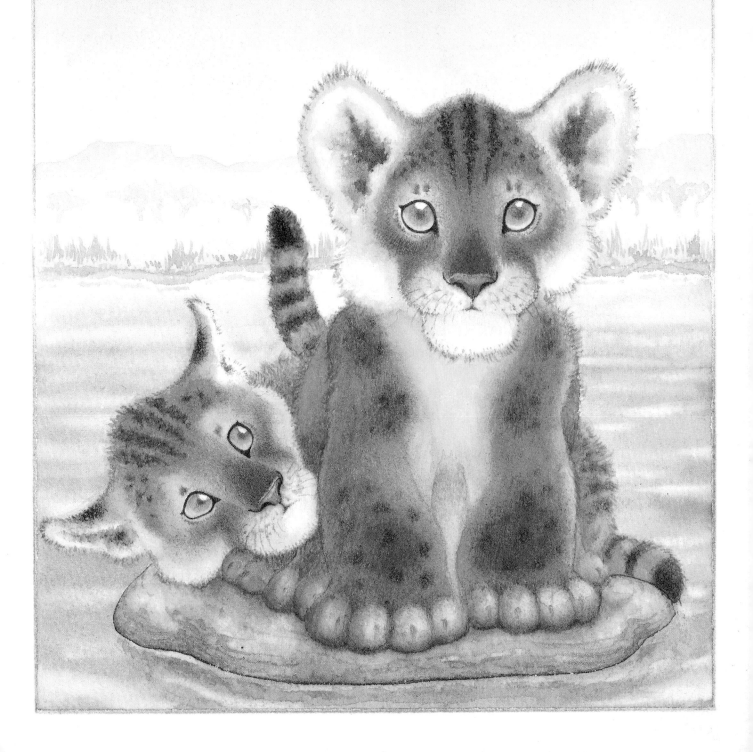

Just at that moment Mum arrived on the bank with
Great Uncle Jiggly Jowls.
"What a brave lion you are!" bellowed Great Uncle
Jiggly Jowls as Jasper led Jake to safety.

"And what a naughty lion you are!" Mum told Jake.

All the way home Mum was angry. Because she'd been anxious.

At supper she was irritable. Because she was relieved. And at bedtime she spoke sternly to Jake. "Now what have you learned today?"

"Not to play by the river. And that there's more to being brave than showing off," mumbled Jake. "Exactly," said Mum. And then she tried to explain.

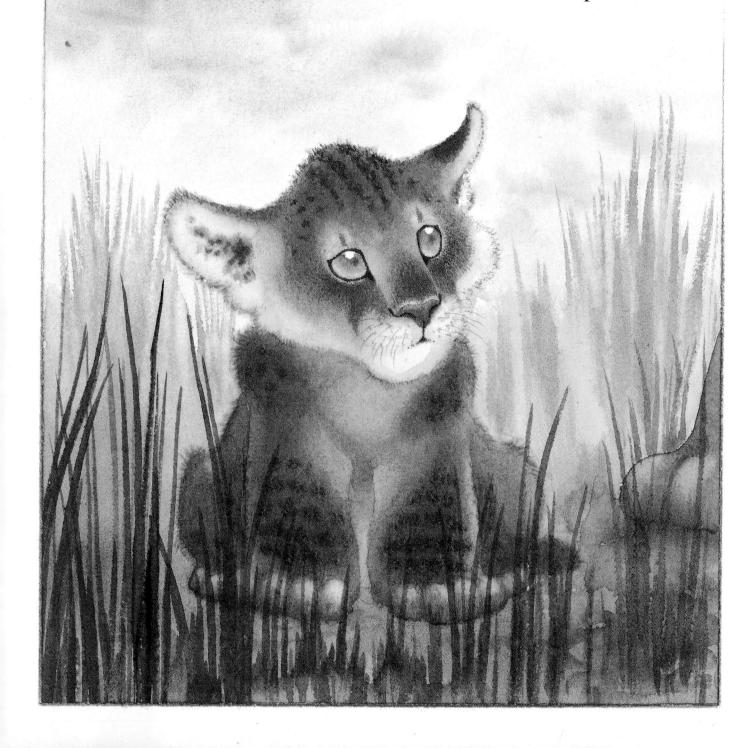

"We all get scared sometimes. And it takes a really brave lion to overcome his fear and act with courage." Jasper wriggled with embarrassment.

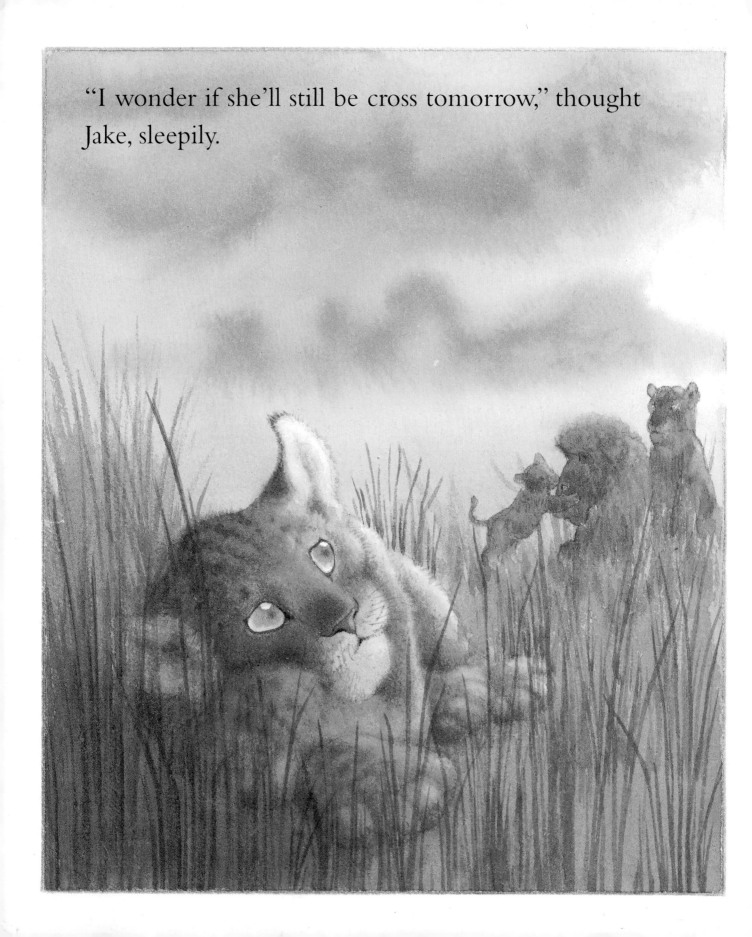

"I wonder if she'll still be cross tomorrow," thought Jake, sleepily.

But, as the sun went down, Mum licked Jake gently behind his ears. She gave Jasper a playful push.

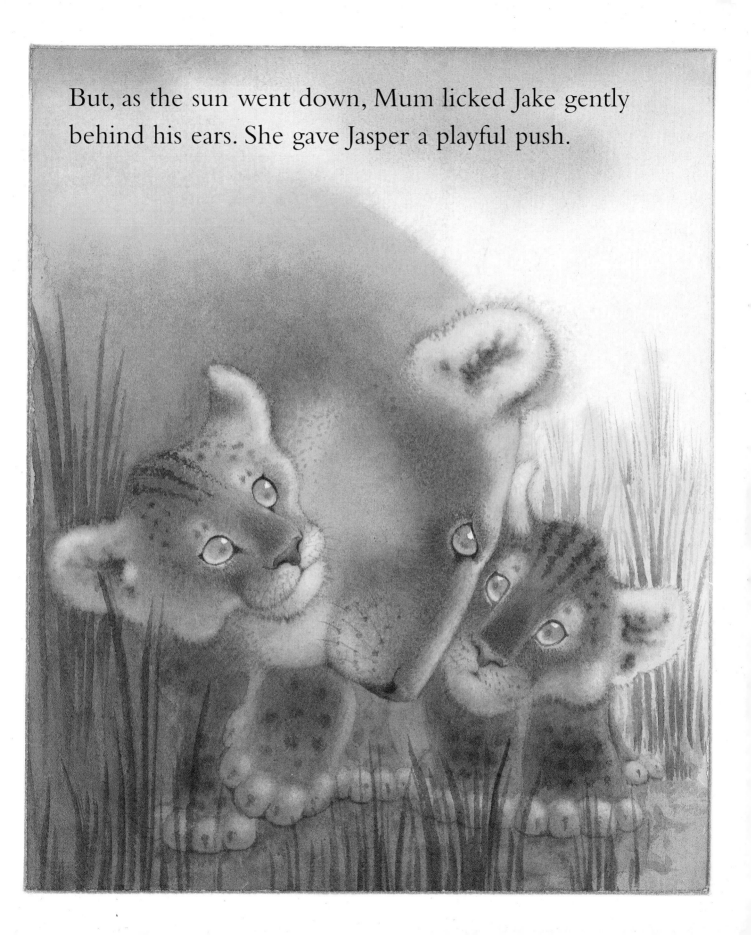

And when the cubs snuggled closer, she said exactly
the same thing to each of them.
"What a special lion you are!"

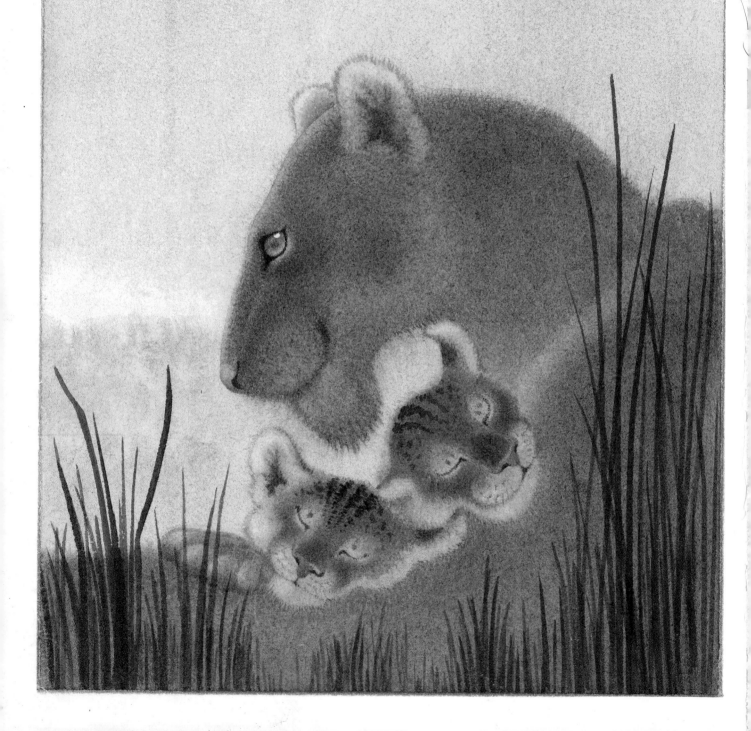